Felice
the Christmas Fairy

by Irene Mathias

illustrated by Anja Uhren

Handersen Publishing, LLC
Lincoln, Nebraska

Handersen Publishing, LLC
Lincoln, Nebraska

Felice the Christmas Fairy

Text copyright © 2017 Irene Mathias
Illustrations copyright © 2017 Anja Uhren
Cover copyright © 2017 Handersen Publishing, LLC
Cover Design by Anja Uhren
Interior Design by Anja Uhren & Nichole Hansen

Manufactured in the United States of America.

Summary: When Felice the Christmas Fairy is knocked down from the tree, it is up to all of the decorations to help her back to the top so they can save the Christmas magic.

Library of Congress Control Number: 2017958410
Handersen Publishing, LLC, Lincoln, Nebraska

ISBN-13: 978-1-941429-952

Publisher Website: www.handersenpublishing.com
Publisher Email: editors@handersenpublishing.com
Author Website: www.betterthancandybooks.com
Illustrator Website: anjauhren.com

For those who believe.
May you always find the magic.

Becky told her mother, as she danced around the tree,

"In the morning there'll be presents here, and every one for me!
I **want** my Christmas stocking to be full of toys and treats.
Santa better not be stingy when he's handing out the sweets!"

"I **want** the chocolates
on the tree and Santa's cookies too,
And I **want** that Christmas Fairy
with her sparkly
silver shoes!"

She pulled and shook the Christmas tree,
Felice tipped to the right,
Just as spoiled little Becky's mother
marched her out of sight.

The house was dark and quiet,
    Claws the cat slipped through the door,
And the breeze that came behind him
    blew Felice onto the floor.
She laid beneath the branches,
    hair a mess, wand snapped in two.
Her crown was topsy-turvy,
    and she'd lost a silver shoe.

But she didn't seem to notice,
    she just smiled and looked around,
For the Christmas Tree looked different
    when she saw it from the ground!

The long green branches sparkled, their tips bejeweled with snow,
And the colours hypnotised her – green, red, blue, gold, indigo.

All the decorations gently twirled above her head,
Snowmen, bells and snowflakes, and a Santa Claus in bed.
Reindeer, elves and polar bears, penguins, angels, stars,
Teddies, holly, candy canes and gingerbread guitars.

She saw each frosty icicle and every twinkling light,
And the sparkling rainbow colours
    made her cheeks glow with delight.
It was a world of pure enchantment
    that Felice had never known,
And she knew within her fairy heart
    she'd love to call it home.

"Pssst," a whisper from the tree.

"Hey Princess, take my hand!"

And a soldier of the lower branches
helped Felice to stand.

"Your Majesty,
we're honoured
for I never thought we'd meet.
All we can see from down here
is a pair of silver feet."

"But we need to get you
back on top,
in case the cat comes back,
Or you'll end up as his plaything,
like my old friend Frosty Jack.

One year he toppled off his branch
and rolled across the floor,
And with lightning speed,
Claws bounded in
and dragged him out the door!"

She looked up high towards the spot
   she sat on every year.
"It's such a long way," sighed Felice,
   "and so much nicer here."

"All I can see from up there
   are the branches long and green,
But underneath it all
   there is this magic I've not seen!"

"Each year I thought I was alone,
   I stood there by myself,
Watching spoiled Becky's family
   put cards up on the shelf."

"Don't send me back up to the top.
   Please, let me stay right here!"
And Felice the Christmas Fairy
   cried a glistening crystal tear.

The Golden Ballerina took her hand,
"Come sit with me."

Then she told her of the magic that Felice brought to the tree.

"You're full of Christmas Spirit.
Santa gave that gift to you.
He placed it in your fairy heart,
your wand and silver shoes.

It flows from you
down through the tree.
It starts there at the top.
And without you being up there, well . . .
. . . the magic will just stop."

"The Christmas decorations
will lose their spark and shine.
Their colours will just melt away,
even yours and mine!"

Felice, now feeling brighter,
had a wonderful idea.

"Hurry!
Get me up there,
before Santa Claus
gets here!
I've something I must ask him,
and I'm sure he will agree.
I think I know how we can keep
the magic
in the tree!"

So the soldier called the Snowman,
and he called the High-branch Elf.

"You'll have to help me
move her.
I can't do it by myself."

"I'll push her
from the bottom.
Snowman, fetch a
candy cane,"

"And hook it round
her middle."

"Pull!"

"Again!"

"Again!"

"Again!"

From the Snowman
to the Reindeer,
to the Penguin
to the Bear,

To the Robin,
then the Eskimo
with snowflakes
in his hair.

They tossed
and pulled
and pushed her
till she stood
beside the Elf,

Who lifted her
and placed her
on the treetop
by himself.

Felice stood very patiently, till Santa Claus got there,
And she watched him eat the cookies from the table by the stair.
As Santa opened up his sack, he took a look around,
And he saw Felice's wand and shoe scattered on the ground.

"Oh, sticky gumdrops!
What a mess!"

He took her off the tree.

"Tell me how this happened!"

And he sat her
on his knee.

So Felice told him the story, and she hoped that he'd agree,
To her plan that might just help to keep the magic in the tree.

She asked if he would help her, and he held Felice up high,
And he sprinkled her with magic from the twinkling in his eye.
He placed her back up on the tree, once more as good as new.

"Of course I'll help," he chuckled,

"and here is what we'll do . . ."

Spoiled Becky woke her mum.

"Come on it's Christmas Day!
I'm not going back to bed to wait,
I don't care what you say!"

"I don't care if it's five o'clock,
move, pronto, on the double,
And you better make me pancakes,
or there really **will** be trouble!"

"Move yourself, let's go downstairs,
in fact, just carry me.
I need to see what Santa Claus
has left beneath the tree!"

She jumped upon her
mother's back,

"Chop-chop,
make it snappy!
Take me
downstairs **now**,
or I'll really be
unhappy!"

The room was filled with presents,
every single one the same.
On each one, tied with ribbon,
hung a tag with Becky's name.

on all the wrapping,
finally lost control,
discovered every parcel
big black lump of coal.

ealed and coughed and spluttered,
she threw the coal around.
om the corner of her eye,
something lying on the ground.
marked "To Becky",
right there on the floor.
shiny, golden star
the table at the door.

Dear Becky,
I've been watching you, I've noticed every day
That your behaviour is disgraceful!
There's nothing more to say.
If you want to make the Nice List
you must rectify your flaws,
Or you'll find more coal beneath your tree.
Merry Christmas
Santa Claus
PS, you can begin
by doing something nice for me.
Please take this star and swap it
for my Fairy on the tree.
Then sit her in the branches,
fix her dress and smooth her hair,
And I will check each Christmas Eve
to make sure she is there.

So Becky did what Santa asked,
  in fact, she did some more.
She tidied all the paper
  and the coal up off the floor.

She listened to her mother – twice –
  but still it was a start,
And she helped to wash the dishes.
  It warmed Santa's heart.

Now every year the golden star
  shines bright from Becky's tree
Felice lives in the branches,
  she's as happy as can be.

Becky rescued Frosty Jack,
    bought Claws a catnip ball.
And now she's on the Nice List,

**Merry Christmas,
one and all!**

Irene Mathias lives in Scotland with her husband and daughter, who is her biggest fan, and also her biggest critic. Irene loves to write poetry and stories for children and she has had success in local, national and international competition with many of her tales. Discover more about Irene and her work at www.betterthancandybooks.com.

Anja Uhren is a storyteller – working with images as well as words to deliver narratives. Originally from Germany, she now lives and works in Sheffield, UK, as a freelance illustrator, after graduating from the Arts University Bournemouth in summer 2015. Anja loves drawing, traveling and comics, and nothing better than combining all three. On her journeys, big and small, she always carries one or two sketchbooks to record observations and impressions which later inform and inspire her illustration practice. To find out more about Anja's work please visit her website – anjauhren.com

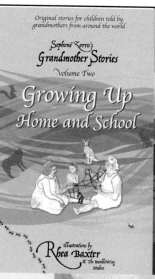
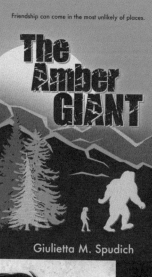

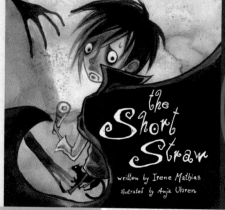
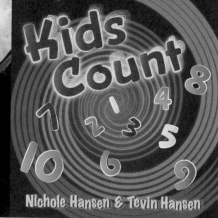
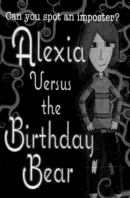

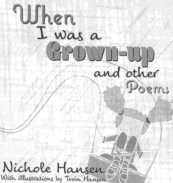
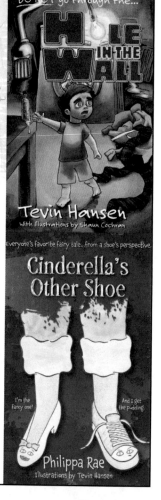

Made in the USA
Middletown, DE
03 December 2020